CW01649226

PRAY

... A Beginner's Guide to Prayer for Kids

Chris Oyakhilome

LET'S PRAY

ISBN 978-978-55333-9-2

Published by LoveWorld Publishing
3, Adebayo Akande Street, Oregun, Ikeja, Lagos, Nigeria.
E-mail: info@kiddiesloveworld.org,
Website: www.kiddiesloveworld.org.

Copyright © 2018 by LoveWorld Publishing.

All rights reserved under International Copyright Law.
Contents and/or cover may not be reproduced in whole or in part in any form without the express written permission of LoveWorld Publishing.

Scripture taken from the New King James Version®.
Copyright © 1982 by Thomas Nelson, Inc. Used by permission. All rights reserved

A KEY FOR OTHER BIBLE TRANSLATIONS USED

MSG	**- The Message Translation**
AMPC	**- The Amplified Classic Bible**
NLT	**- New Living Translation**
GNB	**- GoodNews Bible**

FOR MORE INFORMATION AND TO PLACE ORDERS:

UNITED KINGDOM:
Believers' LoveWorld
Unit C2, Thames View Business Center,
Barlow Way Rainham-Essex,
RM 13 8BT
Tel.: +44 (0) 1708 556 604
Fax.: + 44(0) 2081 816 290

USA
Believers' LoveWorld
4237 Raleigh Street
Charlotte, NC 28213
Tel.: +1 980-219-5150

USA:
Christ Embassy Houston,
8623 Hemlock Hill Drive,
Houston, Texas. 77083
Tel.: +1-281-759-5111;
+1-281-759-6218

CANADA:
Christ Embassy Int'l Office
50 Weybright Court, Unit 43B
Toronto, ON MIS 5A8
Tel.: +1 647-341-9091

SOUTH AFRICA:
303 Pretoria Avenue
Cnr. Harley and Braam Fischer,
Randburg, Gauteng
South Africa.
Tel.: +27 11 326 0971
Fax.: +27 113260972

NIGERIA:
Christ Embassy
Plot 97 Durumi District, Abuja, Nigeria.

LoveWorld Conference Center
Kudirat Abiola Way, Oregun
P.O. Box 13563 Ikeja, Lagos.
Tel.: +234-812-340-6547
+234-812-340-6791

CONTENT

INTRODUCTION

Isn't it great to know God hears you every time you pray? Even if it's just a whisper, God hears it. And if He hears it, you can expect Him to answer too.

God asked us to pray because He loves to hear and answer our prayers. He said, ***"Call me and I'll answer, [I'll] be at your side ..."*** (Psalms 91:15 MSG). That's the joy of prayer.

I once read the story of someone who though had been attending a church for some time, wouldn't give his heart to the Lord, nor say prayers.

One day, while at the meeting, someone asked him why he hadn't been praying. Want to know his response? He said he wasn't sure the folks, with the way they prayed, received answers!

Some kids think that way too. They wonder why they should pray, because they aren't sure if God would hear them.

In this book on prayer, you'll understand what prayer is about, and the benefits of praying. You'll learn how to pray from your heart, the importance of using the Name of Jesus, and so much more.

When you're done reading this book, you would have learnt so much about prayer that it will become one of your favourite things to do!

Happy reading and God bless you!

Pastor Chris Oyakhilome

Chapter One

GOD IS A FATHER

"Is God really a Father?"

Some kids don't know how to relate with God, because they don't know who He really is. They think God lives way up in space, and so it's difficult to have any relationship with Him.

One day, a young boy was asked what he thought about God. "Well, I call God when I need help with things," he replied. "But not my homework, because my mum says I have to do that myself."

You see, God is not just a God who lives way up in space, or One that you call only when you need help. He is a Father and a Friend; One who's close, and can be trusted.

God loves you dearly. He isn't looking to punish you for what you've done wrong. Rather, He loves you and wants you to know it. His love for you is greater than you could ever imagine.

And guess what? He loves you as though you were the only one on earth. He proved His love for you by sending His Son, Jesus, to die for your sins, and to give you a brand new life and nature. The Bible says,

"For God so loved the world that He gave His only begotten Son, that whoever believes in Him should not perish but have everlasting life" (John 3:16).

No matter what you've done, God's love for you is special and greater than the love anyone has for you. You can't compare it with the love your dad, mum or friends have for you. He says in His Word,

"...I've never quit loving you and never will. Expect love, love, and more love" (Jeremiah 31:3 MSG).

So, God doesn't want you to relate with Him as a stranger, He wants to be a Father to you. He wants to have a Father-child relationship with you. However, for God to be your Father, you must be born again. How? By receiving Jesus Christ as your Lord and Saviour.

"...if you confess with your mouth the Lord Jesus and believe in your heart that God has raised Him from the dead, you will be saved. For with the heart one believes unto righteousness, and with the mouth confession is made unto salvation" (Romans 10:9-10).

Say the prayer below aloud to receive Jesus as Lord of your life:

"Dear Lord, I believe with all my heart in Jesus Christ, the Son of the living God. I believe He died for me, and God raised Him from the dead. I believe He's alive today. I confess with my mouth that Jesus Christ is the Lord of my life from this day. Through Him and in His Name, I have eternal life; I'm born again. Thank you Lord, for saving my soul! I'm now a child of God. Hallelujah!"

Congratulations! You're now a child of God, and a member of God's family!

God is excited to have you as His child, and He wants you to have a relationship with Him. One great way you can relate with God is through prayer.

In the next chapters, you'll find how to have a rich fellowship with God through prayer.

ACTIVITIES

Circle the letter with the right answer below

1. **God wants you to relate with Him as______**
   A. a stranger B. a big God up in Heaven
   C. your Father D. a teacher

2. **Complete this sentence, "For God to be your Father______"**
   A. you must pray hard.
   B. you must be born again.
   C. you must attend church meeting.
   D. you must answer to a Christian name.

3. **According to the passage, when you're born again, you become a member of God's_____**

   A. House B. Family C. School D. Choir

4. **Complete this Scripture verse, "*...if you confess with your mouth the Lord Jesus and believe in your heart that God has raised Him from the dead* ______ (Romans 10:9).**
   A. you know the Lord.
   B. you will pray better.
   C. you will go to heaven.
   D. you will be saved.

Chapter Two

WHAT IS PRAYER?

"Isn't prayer all about asking God for my needs?"

Have you ever thought about what prayer is? Some think prayer is all about asking God for what they need; others say, it's a way of getting God to do things for them. They say things like: "Father, I need some clothes," "Lord, it's about time I had a new pair of shoes," "Lord, make my mum take me to the zoo," and so on. Not at all, prayer is much more than that.

Does it then mean you can't ask God for what you need? Sure, you can. You see, asking God for something is a part of prayer. But that isn't all there is to prayer.

For example, the relationship between you and your dad or mum isn't only about asking them for what you want, or telling them to do things for you. It's much more than that. There're times you chat with your dad or mum about your friends, your favourite TV programmes, homework, or the games you participated in at school. In the same way, God wants you to be free to express yourself, and tell Him about anything and everything. This is what you can do through prayer.

So, what then is prayer?

Prayer is fellowship with the Lord, and fellowship is a friendly relationship among people. During prayer, you develop a special relationship with the Lord. This is when you tell Him how much you love Him, the way you feel, or what's on your mind. It's a moment you enjoy a blissful time of conversation with the Lord. That means, you're not the only one talking, He also talks to you, and you listen to Him.

"God is faithful, by whom you were called into the fellowship of His Son, Jesus Christ our Lord" (1 Corinthians 1:9).

So, prayer helps you know the Lord better, and strengthens your relationship with Him. These are some of the reasons prayer is so much fun!

ACTIVITIES

Circle the letter with the right answer below

1. **Some think prayer is all about ____________**
   A. Asking God for whatever they need.
   B. Getting God to do things for them.
   C. Asking God to provide their needs.
   D. All of the above.

2. **Which of these is correct about prayer?**
   A. Prayer is making God love you.
   B. Prayer is fellowship with the Lord.
   C. Prayer is complaining to the Lord.
   D. Prayer is a disturbance to the Lord.

3. **Prayer strengthens your relationship with God.**
   A. True
   B. False
   C. Not Sure
   D. It could be true

4. **Prayer times are special because____________**
   A. You can complain to God about things you don't like.
   B. You can enjoy the Father-child relationship you have with the Lord.
   C. You can get the Lord to do your bidding.
   D. You can make demands and get what you want.

5. **God wants you to be free to express yourself, and tell Him about anything and everything.**
   A. True B. False

Chapter Three

THE LORD LOVES TO HEAR YOU PRAY

"How could God possibly hear me when there're lots of people praying to Him at the same time?"

Some kids think that they'll be bothering God when they pray. "There're lots of people all over the world praying to God at the same time," they say. "How could He possibly hear me?"

They think God is either busy fixing the problems in the world or attending to the long lists of prayer requests, so He wouldn't have the time to hear their own prayer. That isn't true. Don't allow such thoughts into your heart.

God can do many things at the same time, because He is God. He can be talking to someone far away in another part of the world, and at the same time be listening to you, as though you're the only one He's attending to. So, you see, God is never too busy to hear you.

What's more, God doesn't hold something back from you just because someone else had asked Him for the same thing. He doesn't prefer someone else's prayer to yours. God listens to you as though you're the only one praying. And because He's listening, He'll answer too! Wow, isn't that beautiful! So, be mindful that every time you pray, the Lord is willing and happy to grant your request. This is why He said,

"...Ask, and you will receive, that your joy may be full" (John 16:24).

ACTIVITIES

Circle the letter with the right answer below

1. **Which of these statements is correct?**
   A. God can't hear you, because there're lots of people praying to Him at the same time.
   B. God is busy fixing the problems in the world.
   C. God is too busy attending to the long lists of prayer requests.
   D. God is never too busy to hear your prayer.

2. **God can do many things at the same time, because He is God.**
   A. True B. False

3. **Which of these sentences is true?**
   A. God wouldn't give you what you asked for, because another child is asking for the same thing.
   B. God wouldn't give you what you asked for,

because sometimes, it's not easy to get things from Him.

C. God doesn't have the time to hear everybody's prayer.

D. God doesn't hold back from you just because someone else asked Him for what you're asking for.

4. **How does God relate with you when you pray?**

A. He relates with you as though you're the only one He's attending to.

B. He only attends to you when He's done attending to the requests of others.

C. He wants to be sure you really need what you're asking for.

D. God wants you to be done with your prayer as quickly as possible.

5. **Which of these is true?**

A. God is listening but He may not hear your prayer.

B. God is NOT listening, so He will not hear you.

C. God will hear you when you shout your prayer.

D. God is always listening when you pray.

Chapter Four

PRAY FROM YOUR HEART

"How can I pray from my heart?"

Some kids are taught to recite prayers. They even have prayer books from which they recite these prayers. When they are done reciting these prayers, they believe they have prayed.

To recite prayers is to say prayers you have memorised, either from a book or a person. It's easy for your mind to wander off when you recite prayers. You see, to have a rich fellowship with the Lord, you've got to pray from your heart. Praying from your heart makes prayer exciting and enjoyable.

"How do I pray from my heart?" You may ask.

To pray from your heart is to stay focused on what you're praying about. Some kids are easily distracted when praying. You see, prayer time is not the time to think about ice cream or toys, nor is it the time for video games or looking around to see what everyone else is doing. No! Let your heart be in what you're praying for, by concentrating on what you're praying about.

When you stay focused in prayer, it'll be easy to hear from the Lord, and receive answers too. You'll discover that praying is not a religious activity, but a time of intimate fellowship with the Father, who is able to do more than what you ask Him.

No wonder the Bible says,

"The earnest (heartfelt, continued) prayer of a righteous man makes tremendous power available ..." (James 5:16 AMPC).

For me, this is why praying is fun, because I always receive answers when I pray. And as I pray, the Lord speaks to me, and gives me direction on the things I'm doing. This is why I'm very successful in anything I do. You can have this experience too if you take to heart what I'm teaching you in this book.

ACTIVITIES

Circle the letter with the right answer below

1. **What does praying from your heart mean? It means__________**
   - A. to pray aloud.
   - B. to say "the Lord's Prayer."
   - C. to say the prayer that is written in a book.
   - D. to stay focused on what you're praying about, without distractions.

2. **What should you do when you're praying from your heart?**
   - A. Your mind should be focused on what you're saying.
   - B. You should open your eyes to see what's going on around you.
   - C. You should recite the prayers you have memorised from a book.
   - D. You should repeat the same words over and over.

3. **When you pray from your heart__________**
   - A. it'll be easy to hear from the Lord.
   - B. it'll be easy to be distracted.
   - C. it'll be easy to detect how long you've been praying.
   - D. it'll be easy to get tired.

Chapter Five

—THE NAME OF JESUS—

"Does the Name of Jesus really make a difference?"

Praying to the Father in the Name of Jesus is important, because anytime we pray in the Name of Jesus, God hears and answers us. But, you may wonder, "Why do we have to pray in the Name of Jesus?"

The Name of Jesus is all powerful. Its power is not in how it's spelt or pronounced; it's not even in the way it sounds; it's in the One who bears it - JESUS.

Imagine your classmate walked up to you and said, "The Head Teacher asked me to call you." I'm sure you'd immediately hurry along to see your Head Teacher. You would respond in that manner, because you recognised the authority of the Head Teacher.

The Name of Jesus has authority over everything in heaven, on earth and under the earth. That's why His Name is all powerful. The Bible declares that the Name of Jesus is greater than all other names!

"Therefore God also has highly exalted Him and given Him the name which is above every name, that at the name of Jesus every knee should bow, of those in heaven, and of those on earth, and of those under the earth, and that every tongue should confess that Jesus Christ is Lord, to the glory of God the Father" (Philippians 2:9-11).

According to the Bible in Acts 3:1-8, Peter and John were on their way to the Temple to pray when they saw a lame man begging for alms at the Temple gate. This man had never walked in his life! Rather than give him money, Peter gave him something far greater than what he was asking for. Peter said to the poor lame beggar, *"Silver and gold I do not have, but what I do have I give you: in the name of Jesus Christ of Nazareth, rise up and walk!"*

Immediately, the man jumped up and began to walk. The Name of Jesus made the lame man walk again. Hallelujah!

The Name of Jesus is so amazing! You too can use that Name, and have what you want. You can pray for your loved ones, heal the sick, and cast out devils. You can even pray for the children in your neighbourhood and country to know the Lord the way you do, and it will be as you've prayed, glory to God! So, every time you pray in the Name of Jesus, have confidence that God is listening to you, hears and grants what you asked of Him.

ACTIVITIES

Circle the letter with the right answer below

1. **For your prayer to be heard ____________**
   A. You must pray in the Name of Jesus.
   B. You must pray aloud.
   C. You don't have to pray in the Name of Jesus.
   D. You must pray in the name of an angel.

2. **Where is this quote, *"Therefore God also has highly exalted Him and given Him the name which is above every name, that at the name of Jesus every knee should bow, of those in heaven, and of those on earth, and of those under the earth, and that every tongue should confess that Jesus Christ is Lord, to the glory of God the Father,"* from?**
   A. Matthew 2:9-11
   B. Philippians 2:9-11
   C. Philippians 2:30-31
   D. Colossians 2:9-11

3. ***Who spoke to the poor lame beggar at the Temple gate to be healed?____________***
   A. Peter and Paul
   B. Paul and John
   C. Peter
   D. Paul and Silas

Chapter Six

THE RIGHT WAY TO PRAY

"How should I pray using the Name of Jesus?"

Do you know there's a right way to pray? Some kids pray, but they don't see the result of their prayers. They wonder, "Why are my prayers going unanswered when so-and-so always seems to receive everything he asks God for?"

The problem with those who pray and get no answers to their prayers is that they're praying the wrong way; they're ignorant of what the Word says about prayer!

In this chapter, I'll be showing you the right way to pray, so you can enjoy every moment with the Lord in prayer, and always have answers to your prayers.

1. Pray in the Name of Jesus and not through Jesus

There's a big difference between praying ***in* the Name of Jesus** and ***praying through Jesus.***

Praying through Jesus could be likened to you asking your brother or sister to talk to your dad or mum for you. That would be awkward since you can easily walk up to your parents, and talk to them yourself instead of telling someone else to do the talking for you.

You were given direct access to the Father the moment you were born again, so you don't need to ask Jesus to pray to the Father on your behalf. He wants you to talk to the Father yourself.

Before you were saved, you couldn't come to the Father except through Jesus. That's because Jesus is the only way to the Father. Jesus said,

"I am the way, the truth, and the life. No one comes to the Father except through Me" (John 14:6).

Now that you're born again, what you should do is pray to the Father in the Name of Jesus.

"... Most assuredly, I say to you, whatever you ask the Father in My name He will give you" (John 16:23).

When you pray in the Name of Jesus, you're actually using the right and power in that Name; it's as though Jesus Himself is the one praying.

2. Pray to the Father and not to Jesus

The moment you were born again, Jesus became your "Big Brother." So, He doesn't want you praying to Him; rather, He wants you to pray to the Father in His Name.

There's nothing wrong with telling Jesus how much you love Him. You can even worship, praise or give Him thanks for what He's done for you. But you don't pray to Him; rather you pray to the Father in His

Name. So it would be wrong to pray,

"Dear Lord Jesus, I pray you'll heal my sick mum, in Jesus' Name," "Lord Jesus, I ask for a new school bag, in Jesus' Name," "Dear Lord Jesus, I pray for my parents, teachers and friends in Jesus' Name. Amen." etc.

Jesus doesn't want you praying to Him; He tells you to pray to the Father using His Name. That's how to get the Father's attention. And because the Father is listening, He'll answer too. So, when you're praying, follow this simple instruction Jesus gave:

"...You will ask Me nothing. Most assuredly, I say to you, whatever you ask the Father in My name He will give you" (John 16:23).

In summary, when you pray, don't pray to or through Jesus; rather, pray to the Father in the Name of Jesus.

ACTIVITIES

Circle the letter with the right answer below

1. **As a child of God, Jesus is your 'Big Brother.'**

   A. Yes B. No

2. **When you pray in the Name of Jesus, you're actually using the right and power in that Name.**

   A. True
   B. False
   C. Not sure
   D. All of the above

3. **Jesus doesn't want you praying to Him; rather He wants you to pray to the Father in His Name.**

   A. True B. False

4. **Which Scripture verse is, "... *Most assuredly, I say to you, whatever you ask the Father in My name He will give you."*?**

A. John 23:16
B. John 6:23
C. John 16:23
D. John 16:2

5. **The right way to pray is to pray__________**

A. to the Father in the Name of Jesus.
B. through Jesus to the Father.
C. to Jesus in Jesus' Name.
D. to the Father in the name of an angel.

Chapter Seven

DIFFERENT KINDS OF PRAYER

"Are there different kinds of prayer?"

There're different kinds of prayer in the Bible. Let's take a look at just three of them:

1. The Prayer of Intercession

Intercession is from the word, "intercede." It means to speak or plead on behalf of someone.

For instance, imagine that your class teacher came into the class and saw the flower vase on her table was broken. She asked who did it, and the whole class pointed at Tommy, one of your classmates. But just as she was about to tell him off, you stood up and explained that he broke the vase by mistake, and you pleaded on his behalf. Then your class teacher changed her mind. You just interceded on Tommy's behalf.

In the same way, when you intercede in prayer, you're speaking to the Lord on behalf of someone else. As God's child, you have a responsibility to pray for your loved ones, parents, friends, neighbours, and your country. It's an important and precious responsibility.

"... I exhort first of all that supplications, prayers, intercessions, and giving of thanks be made for all men, for kings and all who are in authority, that we may lead a quiet and peaceable life in all godliness and reverence" (1 Timothy 2:1-2).

There're several accounts in the Bible of people who interceded for others. An example was Moses. He interceded for the children of Israel when they sinned, and the Lord forgave them (Exodus 32:31-32). Also, the prayer of the Christians in Jerusalem saved Peter from death, and he was rescued from prison by an angel (Acts 12:3-11).

There're children that are sick in hospitals, some are in orphanages, and there are those who don't have people to care for them. When you intercede for them, through your prayers, you make it possible for God's will to be done in their lives.

2. The Prayer of Agreement

The Prayer of Agreement is when two or more people come together to pray about a particular thing or for someone.

The story of Daniel and his friends in the Bible is a good example of the prayer of agreement.

King Nebuchadnezzar had a puzzling dream; he

commanded all the wise men in his kingdom to tell him the dream and its meaning, but none of them could. This made the king very angry, and he commanded that all his wise men be executed. But when Daniel heard the king's command, he called his three friends, and they prayed about it, and God showed Daniel the dream,

"Then the secret was revealed to Daniel in a night vision. So Daniel blessed the God of heaven" (Daniel 2:19).

Then the king promoted Daniel and made him president over the whole province of his kingdom, and the chief administrator over all the wise men in the kingdom of Babylon. Hallelujah!

3. The Prayer of Thanksgiving

This prayer is about you simply thanking, praising and worshipping the Lord for what He's done for you, your family, friends, church and country.

David was a man who had the attitude of gratitude, and prayed like this a lot.

"It is good to give thanks to the Lord, and to sing praises to Your name, O Most High ... For You, LORD, have made me glad through Your work; I will triumph in the works of Your hands" (Psalm 92:1,4).

The Bible tells the story of a leper who got much more than he expected, because he was grateful. One day, Jesus entered a village where he met and healed ten lepers. They all went away except one of them who returned to thank Jesus, and for that reason, not only was he healed, every part of his body that was affected by the leprosy was made whole (Luke 17:11-19).

Being thankful is an attitude you should cultivate. When you're thankful, you receive more miracles and blessings from the Lord.

Therefore, give the Lord praise, and let your thanksgiving today be a sign of your gratitude for all He's done for you. The Lord deserves all your praise and adoration.

ACTIVITIES

Circle the letter with the right answer below

1. **List the three kinds of prayer discussed in this chapter. The Prayer of**

   i__________ ii____________ and iii____________

2. **Which of these is correct about the Prayer of Intercession?**

   A. You pray to the Lord on behalf of someone else.
   B. You pray for yourself alone.
   C. None of the options is correct.
   D. All of the above.

3. **In the Prayer of Agreement, there must be __**

   A. At least two people.
   B. One person.
   C. It does not really matter if it was you alone.
   D. All of the above.

4. **What do you do when praying the Prayer of Thanksgiving?**

   A. You give God praise and worship Him.
   B. You complain about the things you don't have.
   C. You pray against the bullies in your school.
   D. You pray for other people.

5. **Complete this sentence, *"When you're thankful, you receive*__________**
   A. more miracles and blessings from the Lord.
   B. more power to pray.
   C. gifts from your parents.
   D. new ideas while studying.

Chapter Eight

PRAYER POSTURES

"Do I have to kneel when I pray?"

If I asked you to take a posture to pray, you most likely would prefer to kneel or stand. However, there are other postures of prayer, like sitting, lying down and even lifting up your hands.

Kneeling Posture
(Ephesians 3:14)

Now, the different postures of prayer will not stop God from hearing you; what's important is focusing on what you're praying about. So, whether you're sitting, standing, lying down or lifting up your hands, let your heart be on the Lord, and He'll hear and answer you. The Lord said,

"When you pray, I will answer you. When you call to me, I will respond..." (Isaiah 58:9 GNB).

There are several postures you can take when praying.

Let's see a few of them.

Standing Posture
(Mark 11:25)

Sitting Posture
(2 Samuel 7:18)

Lying Posture
(Psalm 149:5)

Lifted Hands Posture
(1 Timothy 2:8)

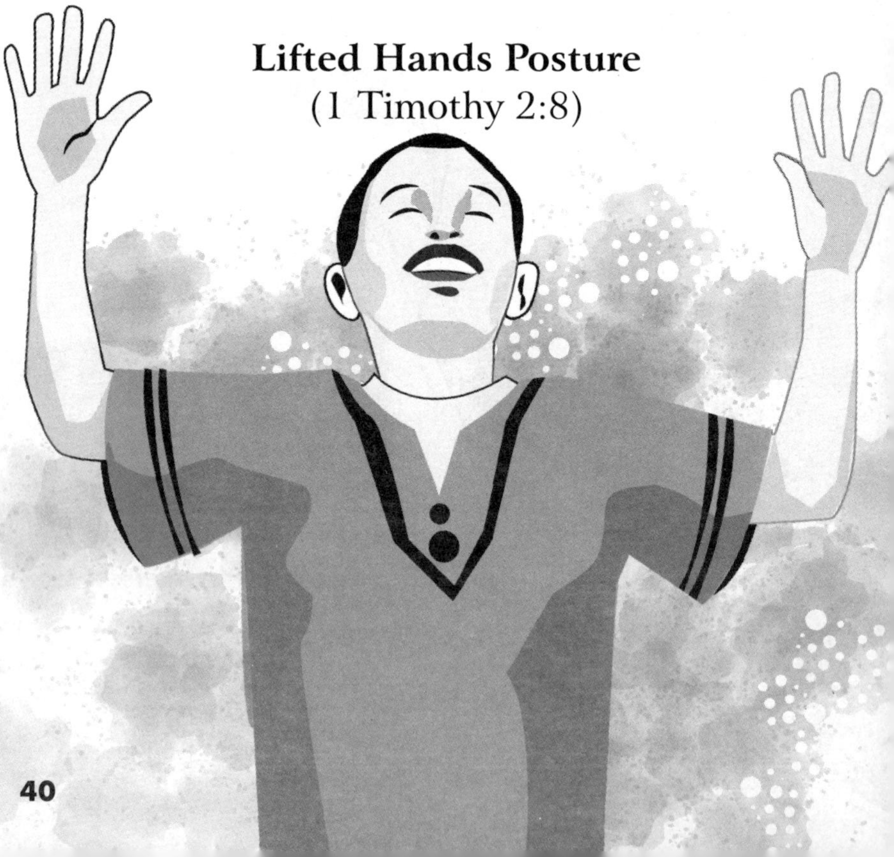

ACTIVITIES

Circle the letter with the right answer below

1. Would your prayer posture prevent God from answering your prayer?
   A. Yes, It would.
   B. No, it wouldn't.
   C. Sometime, it would.
   D. Most times, it wouldn't.

2. How many postures were mentioned in this chapter?
   A. Four B. Five C. Six D. Seven

3. Complete this quote from Isaiah 58:9 (GNB), "When you pray, I will answer you. When you call to me, ________ "
   A. I will hear but will not answer.
   B. I will respond.
   C. I will not hear you.
   D. I will come to you.

4. Without looking into your book, can you say the different kinds of posture discussed in the book?

5. Now that you've learnt so much about prayer, what new things will you do when you pray? List them below:

   ____

   ____

   ____

Chapter Nine

MODEL PRAYERS FOR YOU

"It's time to pray."

Now that you've learnt how to pray, you need to put what you've learnt to practice immediately. This is your moment, and the Lord is eager to hear you pray. In Jeremiah 33:3 (GNB), He says to you,

"Call to me, and I will answer you; I will tell you wonderful and marvelous things that you know nothing about."

Below are model prayers that'll guide you and help you form the right words when you pray:

A Model Prayer for Yourself

Dear Father, I thank you for your Word that I've received through this book. I received it with gladness and faith. I'm strengthened to put all I have learnt to work. I declare that as I put your Word to work, it produces the right results in me, in Jesus' Name.

Thank you Lord, for blessing me. I'm blessed in my spirit, soul and body. I'm blessed in my going out and my coming in. I have a sound mind, I walk in excellence, success and victory. I prosper in everything I do, in the Name of Jesus.

Thank you Lord, for your wisdom is working in me, making me think, speak and act the right way. I walk in grace, because the knowledge of God's Word has increased in my life. I live a life of favour. I'm walking in the blessing and in the glory of the Lord, in the Name of Jesus. Amen.

A Model Prayer of Intercession for Your Country

Dear Lord, I thank you for bringing my attention to prayers for our country. I pray that your peace will continuously reign in our country, and that you'll grant our leaders the grace and wisdom to lead our great nation in the right manner and in the direction of your will. I pray that you'll grant them the boldness to govern our affairs in righteousness and justice, so that the citizens may live their lives in godly fear and reverence, in the Name of Jesus.

I declare that the Gospel has free course throughout our country and the Word of God grows mightily and prevails everywhere. I pray your children are bold to stand up for the Word, and preach it with great power and grace all over this land; and souls are won into the Kingdom daily, in Jesus' Name.

I rebuke every spirit that seeks to cause violence and destruction in our families, cities, states and provinces. I demand that they stop their operations and plots within our borders, in Jesus' Name.

I declare the praise of God, and the knowledge of God's Word is springing forth all over the land, and the gospel prospers to the ends of the earth, in Jesus' Name. Amen.

A Model Prayer of Agreement

Dear Father, your Words says, 'If two of you shall agree on earth as touching anything that they shall ask, it shall be done for them.' Thank you for the privilege of praying in agreement with other believers.

We pray for fellow Christians around the world, that their faith would be strengthened in the Lord that they may grow more and more in grace and in the knowledge of our Lord Jesus Christ.

We pray on behalf of those who are being persecuted for the sake of the Gospel, and those who suffer from injustice that they are strengthened by the power of the Holy Spirit.

We pray for those who are sick and in hospitals. We declare they are healed and restored to health. We agree that their conditions are reversed for good to conform to your Word, in Jesus' Name.

We stand against the works of the devil in our families, schools and countries; and declare they are frustrated in the mighty Name of Jesus. Amen.

A Model Prayer of Thanksgiving

Dear Father, I worship you today for you alone are glorious and worthy of all praise and honour. You're the healer, the provider, and supplier of all good things. Your Name is great and your dominion is everlasting. Your love, mercies and compassion fill the earth! You're glorified in my life, and in all the earth, in Jesus' Name.

Thank you for bringing me forth into a life of continuous victory! I worship you today from the bottom of my heart for your love, kindness, grace and tender mercies! Great and mighty are your works in my life and wondrous are your ways. You are my light and my salvation; you are the strength of my life.

I give you thanks and praise for you have made my life beautiful. I'm excellent, I'm healthy, I'm smart, and I'm blessed and favoured. And by you, I shall yet do greater things and prevail, Hallelujah!

I celebrate your Word at work in me. I rejoice because you have given me eternal life. I rejoice over the Name of Jesus; the Name above all names. Daily, my spirit is opened to offer to you the sacrifice of praise, which is the fruit of my lips, giving thanks and glory to your Name, forever and ever, in Jesus' Name. Amen.

This is a good way to start, but remember, it's only just a start. As you study God's Word, you'll discover that your choice of words will continually improve.

Rhapsody of Realities for Early Readers is a great material to use in your personal study every day. It has inspiring messages, faith-filled confessions and prayers that will help you have a rich fellowship with the Lord.

Now, you can enjoy an ever joyous and victorious life in Christ, as you pray the right way.

ACTIVITIES

Now make these faith-filled confessions:

I'm a champion in this life. I'm favoured and I'm victorious. I'm making progress, I'm moving forward and upward only in my life, in the Name of Jesus.

I'm a success. I'm excellent in all I do, because I have an excellent spirit.

The wisdom of God is working in me mightily, therefore I'll never miss my way. The knowledge of God is increasing in my life, and I'm growing in grace!

Greater is He that is in me than he that is in the world. I'm an overcomer. I'm more than a conqueror.

The glory of God is risen upon me. God lives in me; therefore, I'm strengthened, energized, endued with power, ability and might.

My future is bright and glorious, I cannot fail nor be defeated. I'm super-favoured, I live in abundance because I'm God's child. Hallelujah!